Saturdays are superhéroe days for Abuela and me.
Super hugs! Check.
Super shakes! Clink.
Super capas! Ready.

LET'S SAVE THE WORLD!

CLINK!

BAM!

POW!

Abuela's eyes shine like estrellas.
Together, we shout,
"Super Luis on the job!
"Sidekick Abuela is lista!"

We rescue citizens from danger.

BUMP!

We catch cupcake criminales.

We secure lost capas from tiny intruders.
"No, Isabel!" I say. "You're too little."

Six days until Sidekick Abuela is back.
Five, four, three, two, one, and
¡Viva! It's superheroe day again!
I build our fuerte and even spritz invaders away
with Abuela's super lavanda spray. But Abuela never comes.

"Abuela is not feeling well," Mami says. "She's at the hospital."

"We'll see her tomorrow," Papi says.
"Abuela needs my super hugs," I say.

The next day, I'm ready to see Abuela.
   I climb on the bed and give her a super hug and powerful kisses.
   Abuela smiles.

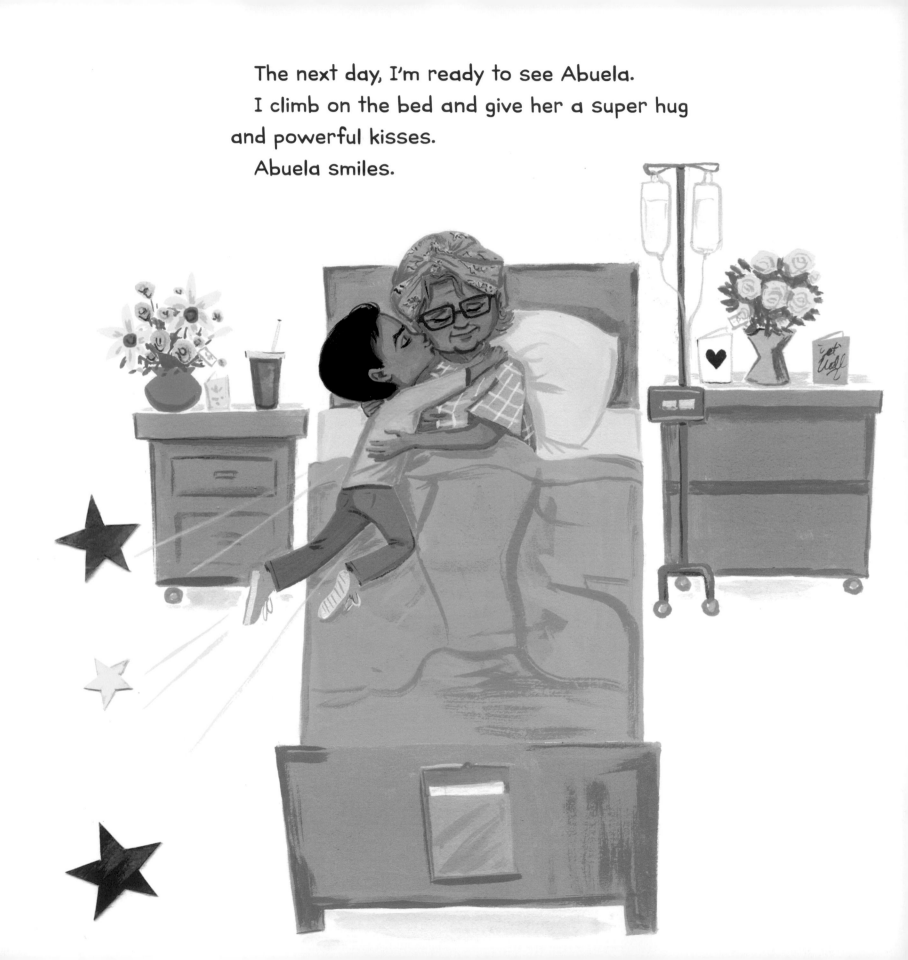

The tiny intruder hugs Abuela, too.
I don't say anything.
Because maybe Abuela needs an extra hug today.

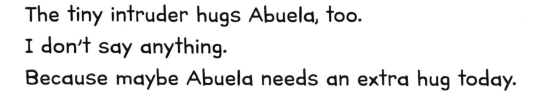

After lots of hugs,

kisses,

and shakes . . .

Abuela comes home to me!
I fly to her arms.
But Abuela is not superhéroe ready.
Papi says she needs to rest.

Rest? For how long?

When can I have my sidekick back?

Maybe I can speed up her recovery with my super poderes.

I light our superhéroe fuerte,

wrap her in my super hugs,

give her sips of our super shake,

and smooch her with power-boosting kisses.

I do everything superhéroes do, but . . .

Abuela doesn't get better.
She tries, but she doesn't look super.
Hmm . . .
My capa makes me stronger.
Maybe that's what she needs.

"Luis, Abuela needs to hang up her capa," Mami says.
"Keep it safe for me, Super Luis," Abuela whispers.
My super vision goes cloudy.
Mami says even supehéroes cry sometimes.

I lie down under our super fuerte.

Isabel invades it.

I let her stay this time.

Mami gives me some super shake.
It doesn't make me strong.

Papi brings me my capa.
"This capa is broken!"
I throw it across the room.

I need my sidekick. I need my Abuela.
She wraps me in a soft squeeze.
I hug double tight, for me and for her.

Isabel dashes into the room.
"¡Abuela! The villains are trying
to steal the super capas!"

I seize Abuela's capa.
But when I hand it to her,
she shakes her head.

"It's okay, Abuela!" I say. "Even if you can't be my sidekick, you'll always be my super Abuela."
And then I see . . .

Isabel is playing with my capa.
"No, Isabel . . ."

Abuela's eyes shine like estrellas.
And I know just what to do.

"This capa is perfecta for you."
I wrap my capa around Isabel.

Then Abuela
gently wraps her
capa around me.

Our eyes shine.
Together, we shout,
"Super Luis on the job!
"Sidekick Isabel is ready, lista!"

GLOSSARY

Abuela—grandma
capa—cape
criminales—criminals
estrellas—stars

fuerte—fort
lavanda—lavender
listo/lista—ready
Mami—mother

Papi—father
perfecta—perfect
poderes—powers

superhéroe—superhero
¡Vámonos!—Let's go!
¡Viva!—Hooray!